First published as a limited edition for W H Smith by
HarperCollins*Publishers,* 1999

This revised and extended edition is published by the
Sharpe Appreciation Society, 2002

The Sharpe Appreciation Society
PO Box 168
West Chatham,
MA, 02669
USA

www.bernardcornwell.net

The author asserts the moral right to be identified as the author of this work.

Printed and bound by McClafferty Printing Company

ISBN 978-0-972222-0-0-6

Introduction

Sharpe's Skirmish was first written in 1998 and written in a great hurry. It should probably not have been written at all because it caused nothing but trouble.

A leading British bookseller devised the idea of giving away a Sharpe short story with every copy of *Sharpe's Fortress* and, at the time, it seemed like a good idea and so I wrote *Sharpe's Skirmish,* but it only upset all the other booksellers who did not have copies of the tale to give to their customers, and then some branches decided they could make money by selling the booklet instead of giving it away, and so a great deal of unhappiness resulted. Only a few thousand were printed, and that was not enough, and it is hardly a surprise that the experiment has never been repeated. *Sharpe's Skirmish* faded away, though copies do crop up from time to time in second hand shops where they fetch an outrageous price. Anyone unwilling to pay for the original booklet could find the story on the internet, but not everyone likes reading from a computer screen and so we are re-issuing the story in a more accessible form.

It was, as I said, written in a tearing hurry. The bad idea came very late, just before *Sharpe's Fortress* was distributed to the shops, and I had only four days in which to find a subject and write the tale. That haste showed, and so this edition is entirely rewritten. It is considerably longer than the first edition and some of the more obscure passages have been cleaned up and made plain. The references to Gawilghur in the tale refer, obviously, to the events described in *Sharpe's Fortress*. Some readers always want to know where Sharpe's stories occur within the greater scheme of his life, so they should know that this small adventure comes after *Sharpe's Sword*.

This edition is being published by the Sharpe Appreciation Society and the proceeds will contribute to the society and to the Bernard and Judy Cornwell Foundation. The Sharpe Appreciation Society exists not just to celebrate Richard Sharpe's adventures, but also to increase awareness of the soldiers who fought through Portugal, Spain and France in the early years of the nineteenth century and we hope that the funds raised will help make possible the society's newsletter and its many visits to battlefields and museums. More information can be found at www.southessex.co.uk. The Bernard and Judy Cornwell Foundation is a charity that concentrates on scholarships for young people.

SHARPE'S SKIRMISH

"Welcome to San Miguel, Captain," Major Lucius Tubbs said to the officer beside him, "where God is in his heaven and all is well with the world."

"Amen to that," said Sergeant Patrick Harper, standing behind the two officers who both ignored him. Major Tubbs, befitting his name, was a plump man with a cheerful, jowly face who now stood on the ramparts of the small fortress of San Miguel and bounced his hands on the parapet in time to some imaginary music. Next to him, and towering above him, was a lean and scarred man in a green Rifleman's jacket that was so patched with common brown cloth that from a distance it looked like a farm-labourer's coat. Beneath the patched coat the Rifleman wore a pair of leather-trimmed cavalry overalls that had once belonged to a colonel of Napoleon's Imperial Guard while at his side there hung a heavy-bladed cavalry sword that had killed the colonel.

"We shall not be disturbed here, Sharpe," Tubbs continued happily.

"Pleased to hear that, sir," Sharpe said.

"The French are gone!" The Major waved a hand which suggested the French had simply evaporated, "which means we shall be unmolested as we do our work in these Elysian fields!" Sharpe had no idea what an Elysian field was and he had no intention of asking, but it was plainly a pleasant sort of place for the landscape beyond the

9

river was gentle, peaceful and bathed in Spanish sunlight. "There is just you and I," Tubbs went on enthusiastically, "our splendid men, and enough wine in the store room to float a frigate." He turned a beaming smile on Sharpe. "Choice wine, no less! In bottles instead of skins."

"Amen to that, too," Sergeant Harper said.

Sharpe turned on him. "Sergeant? Take three reliable men and break every damned bottle."

"Sharpe!" Tubbs remonstrated, staring at the Rifle officer as though he could not believe his ears. "Break the bottles?"

Sharpe looked down into Tubbs's eyes. "The Crapauds may have gone, sir," he said, "but the war ain't won yet. And if a troop of mon-sewers were to come down that road," he pointed south along the road which led from the bridge that the small fortress guarded, "then you and I don't want to be relying on a pack of piss-eyed soldiers who are so damned drunk that they won't be able to load a gun, let alone fire one."

Tubbs looked southwards, seeing nothing but unharvested fields, groves of olives, well tended vineyards, white farmhouses and bright red poppies. "But there are no Frenchmen!" The Major protested.

"Not a one, sir," Harper valiantly backed up the Major.

"There are always damned frogs," Sharpe insisted. "It won't be till we've cleared the world of the last bloody one that you can claim there are no frogs."

"But breaking the bottles, Sharpe!" Tubbs said reprovingly. "It's good wine, I told you! It's bottled, not kept in skins." He saw his words were making no impression on the tall Rifleman. "And doubt-less," he continued, advancing his best argument, "the wine is private property. Have you thought of that? We cannot be responsible for the destruction of private property, Sharpe! There are laws!" The Major waited for Sharpe's agreement, saw it was not coming, so tried another approach. "Why don't we just leave the door locked, eh? Two good padlocks? A reliable sentry?"

Sharpe shook his head. "There ain't one of my men, sir, and I dare say there ain't one of yours, what can't get through a brace of pad-locks in half a minute. And I doubt you'll find a sentry who can't be bribed with a swallow of good bottled wine." He stood gazing down the road beyond the bridge and, so long as Sharpe said nothing more,

Harper stayed stubbornly where he was and Major Tubbs racked his brains for some new reason that would keep the wine safe, then Sharpe suddenly frowned as if a new idea had come to him. "What kind of store-room is it, sir?" he asked, turning back to Tubbs.

"Very like a cellar," the Major said enthusiastically, hoping the question was evidence that Sharpe's resolve was weakening, "the floor is below ground level and the ceiling's a good eight feet above, but it's all stone built. Well built, too, with an arched ceiling and all very secure."

"Stone floor, sir?"

"Oh, indeed! Indeed. It's the only original room left in the castle, you see? The newer accommodation is all made from timber."

Sharpe turned on Harper. "Sergeant, fetch the bottles from the store-room and break them on the bridge." If the fort's store-room was below ground level and stone-flagged Sharpe did not want it flooded with wine, for he knew his men would get down on hands and knees to lap it up, so instead he would have the bottles broken where he could see the wine draining safely into the river. "Do it now!" He snapped at an obviously reluctant Sergeant Harper.

Major Tubbs sighed, but he dared not countermand the order. He was a Commissary Officer who worked for the Storekeeper of the Ordnance, and though he wore a blue-coated uniform that was generously decorated with silver braid, and though he was accorded the courtesy rank of Major, in truth he was a civilian. His job was to help keep the army supplied with muskets, powder and shot, and Lucius Tubbs had never seen a battle, while the dark-haired, much scarred man beside him had lived through too many. Captain Richard Sharpe had once been Private Richard Sharpe and he had made the leap from the ranks to the officer's mess because he was good at war, frighteningly good, and Tubbs, though he would never have admitted it, was more scared of Captain Sharpe than he was of the French.

"Sergeant?" Tubbs called after Harper who was going down the steps from the high rampart, "we might save a few bottles, perhaps? For medicinal reasons?" Tubbs made the suggestion nervously, glancing at Sharpe. "Does not the good book entreat us to 'take a little wine for thy stomach's sake'?" Tubbs pleaded.

"Two dozen bottles in my room, Sergeant," Sharpe said, "for my tummy's sake, and that's all."

"Two dozen it is, sir," Harper said and went on down the stairs.

"Only two dozen?" Tubbs pleaded.

"When it comes to bottles of liquor, Major," Sharpe said, "Sergeant Harper can't count. There'll be six dozen in my room, and as many again hid somewhere else, but if I don't make a point of breaking the rest then the boys will think this is a tavern." He saw doubt on the Major's face. "For God's sake, sir, half the bastards only took the King's shilling because they were promised a pint of rum a day. They don't fight for glory, sir, they fight to get liquor. You want our men to be cross-eyed with wine? We can't afford it, sir, we've got work to do."

Or rather Major Tubbs had work, and to do it he had three Spanish labourers and one Scotsman, Mister MacKeon, who was a Foreman of the Ordnance, which meant that MacKeon would do all the work and Tubbs would take the credit for it because that was the way of the world. Not that much credit would ensue from MacKeon's efforts, but in their small way they would help win the war against the French who, a month before, had been whipped at Salamanca. Arthur Wellesley, now the Viscount Wellington of Talavera, had bamboozled the French, dazzled them, unbalanced them and then half destroyed them. So the frogs had gone. They had marched north with their tails between their legs, and the French garrison of the tiny riverside fort of San Miguel had run with them, but they had left behind, locked in the fort's store-room, close to five thousand muskets.

The priest of San Miguel de Tormes discovered the muskets after the French had left. The weapons had been intended for Marshal Soult's army in the south, but the cavalry regiment which should have escorted the convoy across the Sierra de Gredos had never turned up and then, in the manner of armies, the weapons were forgotten and the garrison commander had put them in the store-room where the priest had found them. The priest had also discovered the wine locked away with the guns and, being an honest man, he had padlocked the store-room and sent word to the British, and now Major Tubbs had arrived to take possession of the muskets. The Major's job was to make sure the guns were all serviceable, after which they would be cleaned, oiled and given to the guerilleros who harassed and ambushed and terrified the French forces occupying Spain. Sharpe, and his Light Company of the South Essex, were charged with the duty of guarding Tubbs's men while they did their work.

But guard Tubbs's men against what? Sharpe doubted there was a Frenchman within a hundred miles of this bridge across the River Tormes. Marmont, beaten at Salamanca, was retreating northwards, while Marshal Soult was pinned south of the River Guadiana by General Hill. In truth, Sharpe thought, the two officers and fifty three men of his Light Company could drink good bottled wine from now until MacKeon finished his work and it would probably make no difference to the war, but Sharpe had not stayed alive by making assumptions of safety. The frogs might have been defeated at Salamanca, they might have their tails between their legs and be far away, but they were not yet beaten.

He ran down the fort's stairs, crossed the courtyard and walked out of the gate onto the bridge where Patrick Harper and three riflemen had just begun the melancholy task of smashing the wine bottles. The Light Company, resting on the bridge, was protesting the destruction and, though the louder voices ceased as soon as Sharpe appeared, the company still let him know their feelings by thumping the butts of their rifles and muskets on the stones of the roadway. Most of the men wore red jackets with the yellow facings of the South Essex regiment, but a score of them were in green coats and those were Riflemen, the survivors of Sharpe's old company who had been melded into the South Essex that was now the only regiment in the line that had both smooth bore muskets and rifled longarms, redcoats and green jackets. The muskets and rifles were now being thumped in the age old expression of disapproval but the sound faded as Sharpe strode to the centre of the bridge. He stared southwards, then turned. "Lieutenant Price!" He called.

"Sir?" The lanky Price had been resting in the shade of a wayside chapel built at the bridge's northern end and now jerked up as though he had been woken.

"I saw some strange uniforms among those vines," Sharpe pointed south across the river and down the long white road which stretched towards the Sierra de Gredos. "The vineyard beside that farmhouse where the windmill is, see it?"

Price hurried to join Sharpe in the centre of the bridge from where he peered southwards. "The far vineyard, sir?" He asked in disbelief.

13

"The very far vineyard," Sharpe confirmed. "Sergeant Harper and his three men will stay here, but you take the rest of the company and search for the bastards. Looked like a dozen of them."

Price frowned. "But if they see us coming, sir, they'll run away." He smiled winningly. "A dozen men can't threaten us, sir. And they're probably partisans, sir, on our side."

"You think they'll run away?" Sharpe asked. "I wouldn't run away from you, Harry, so why should they? On your feet, all of you! You've got work!" He raised his voice, stirring the company who were dust-stained, sweat soaked and exhausted. They had been marched back from Wellington's advancing army for this duty and they had been on the road for two long days and all they wanted now was to drink, sleep, and drink again. "Sergeant Huckfield!" Sharpe called. "Form the company! Sharply, now! Don't want those rascals escaping!"

Lieutenant Price was standing on the bridge parapet to stare at the vineyard that lay at least two miles away across a dry landscape shimmering in the summer heat. "I don't see anyone there, sir," he said helpfully. "Maybe they were there a few moments ago, sir, but not now."

"Go!" Sharpe shouted. "Don't let the bastards get away! Hurry! At the double!" He watched the company leave, then turned to Harper. "Is that the fastest you can break those damned bottles, Sergeant?" Harper and his three men were fetching the bottles from the store room, then stacking them beside the wayside shrine which was a small stone building about ten foot square with a plaster Madonna inside, and only then carrying them one at a time to the bridge parapet where Harper reluctantly broke them. "A spavined cripple could smash them faster than you," Sharpe snarled.

"Maybe he could, sir," the big Irishman said, "but you wouldn't be wanting us to be slipshod, now would you, Captain? Must do a thorough job, sir. Have to make sure each one's properly broken." He tapped a bottle on the parapet. "And you wouldn't want broken glass on the road, sir, now would you."

"Just get on with it," Sharpe snapped, then climbed back up to the fort's parapet where Tubbs was watching the Light Company march southwards.

"Did I hear you say that you saw uniforms, Sharpe?" Tubbs asked

14

anxiously. He was gazing south across the river through a small telescope. "Did you say there was an enemy to the south? Surely not. Surely not here!"

"Didn't see a damn thing, Major," Sharpe said. "But if they've got enough energy to make a protest, they've got energy to go for a march. Don't want them getting slack, do we?"

"Oh, no," Tubbs said weakly, "no, we wouldn't want that." He turned to look at the small village of San Miguel de Tormes that lay close to the fort on the river's northern bank. The village was not much of a place; a couple of dozen houses, a small church, an olive press and the inevitable tavern, one of a hundred such villages on the wide plain that stretched north and south of the river. Heat shimmered above olives and vines. Across the river Lieutenant Price's men marched slowly, their feet kicking up a plume of white dust. A similar smear of white showed in the heat-hazed air just beyond a small grove of trees that straddled the Salamanca road to the north. Major Tubbs saw it first and tentatively touched Sharpe's elbow to point out the white cloud drifting from the road. "Is that smoke, Sharpe?" The Major asked.

"Dust, sir," Sharpe said.

"Dust?"

"Kicked up by boots, sir, or by hooves."

"Dear me!" Tubbs looked alarmed and trained his telescope on the small grove of trees.

"It won't be Frenchmen, sir," Sharpe reassured the Major, "not coming from Salamanca."

"They certainly don't look friendly," Tubbs said anxiously, "whoever they are." He was staring at a band of horsemen who had just emerged from the grove of cork oaks. There were some twenty men in the band, most in wide-brimmed hats and all bristling with weapons. They had muskets slung on their shoulders or holstered in their saddles, sabres and swords hanging beside their stirrups, and pistols stuck into their belts. None was in uniform, though a few wore scraps of old French equipment. Tubbs shuddered. The Major did not consider himself an inexperienced man, indeed he reckoned he had seen more of the world than most folk, yet he had rarely seen such a murderous gang of cut-throat savages. One rider had a great axe slung beside his saddle and another carried the loops of a long

15

black whip and all of them rode confidently, masters of their world, proud and dangerous, and as they drew nearer Tubbs could see that their faces were scarred, moustached, sun-darkened and unsmiling. "Guerilleros?" He suggested to Sharpe.

"Like as not, Major," Sharpe agreed.

Tubbs sighed. "I know they're supposed to be on our side, Sharpe, but I can never find it in my heart to trust them. They're little more than bandits."

"That's very true, sir."

"They're cut-throats!" Tubbs went on, encouraged by Sharpe's agreement, "rogues and criminals! Do you know, Sharpe, they're not even above slitting a British straggler's throat for the value of his equipment!"

"So I've heard, sir."

"And we give them weapons," the Major observed sadly. "We encourage them." He suddenly lowered his telescope as an idea struck him, an idea so horrible that he looked aghast at Sharpe. "You don't suppose, Sharpe," he said anxiously, "that the wine belongs to these rogues, do you?"

"I doubt it, sir," Sharpe said. The wine was almost certainly French plunder, stolen from the vineyards that surrounded the castle and village of San Miguel, and the wine's original owner had probably died when the frogs pillaged his property.

"My God, man!" Tubbs said, "but if the wine does belong to those rogues, they'll be furious! Furious! Call your men back!" Tubbs turned to look for the retreating Light Company, then swivelled back to to gaze at the horsemen. "Suppose they want payment for the wine, Sharpe? What do we do?"

"We tell them to bugger off, sir."

"We tell them to . . . Oh, my God!" Tubbs was alarmed because one of the riders had broken away from the group and was now spurring towards the fortress. He raised his glass again, stared for a few heartbeats, then looked astonished. "Good Lord!"

"What is it, sir?" Sharpe asked calmly.

"It's a woman, Sharpe, a woman!" Tubbs sounded quite faint with surprise. "It's a woman, it truly is and she's armed!" Tubbs was gazing at a thin-faced, good-looking young woman who now trotted towards the small fortress with a gun on her back and a sword at her

16

side. She swept off her hat as she approached, loosing a torrent of long black hair. "A woman!" Tubbs exclaimed again.

Sharpe had levelled his own telescope. "She's rather beautiful, sir," he said.

"They're the worst kind, Sharpe, the very worst! Believe me! Jezebel, Delilah, Salome, they were all of them quite beautiful and utterly murderous!"

"That one's murderous, sir," Sharpe said, lowering his telescope. "She's called La Aguja. Which means 'the needle', and that ain't because she's handy with the cotton and thread, sir, but because she likes to kill with a stiletto."

"She likes to kill with a . . ." Major Tubbs seemed to think he had not heard right. "Do you know her, Sharpe?"

"I'm married to her, Major," Sharpe said, and went down the stairs to greet Teresa.

And reflected that, maybe, whatever they were, he was in the Elysian Fields after all.

§§§

Major Pierre Ducos was no more a proper Major than was Lucius Tubbs, but nor was he quite a civilian either, though he did wear civilian clothes. If forced to describe himself he would probably have answered with false modesty and claimed to be a mere *fonctionnaire,* a humble servant of the Emperor, but few functionaries had minds as exquisitely subtle as Ducos's and none wielded as much influence over the Emperor. "What he is," Marshal Soult had warned his officers against underestimating Pierre Ducos, "is a serpent." *Un serpent,* and a poisonous one at that, though at first glance he appeared quite innocuous. He was a small man, balding and slight, who wore thick spectacles and he might have been taken for a clerk, or perhaps a scholar, except that his sober clothes were too well tailored and too expensive for a man who earned his living with books and pens, and then there were his eyes. They might be short-sighted, but they were also as cold and green as a northern sea, suggesting that mercy and pity were qualities long discarded by Major Pierre Ducos. Pity, Ducos considered, was an emotion fit only for women, while mercy was the prerogative of God, and the Emperor deserved sterner virtues than those of women and God. The Emperor needed efficiency, dedication and intelligence, and Ducos supplied all three, which was why he had the Emperor's ear. He might be a mere Major, but Marshals of France worried about Ducos's opinion, because that opinion could go straight to Napoleon himself.

And Napoleon had sent Ducos to Spain because the Marshals were failing. They were being beaten! They were losing eagles! The armies of France, faced by a rabid pack of Spanish peasants and a despicable little British army, were being trounced and Ducos's responsibility was to analyse those defeats and inform the Emperor what might be done, and every French Marshal and General knew that Ducos's opinion was the key to the Emperor's favour which was why the Generals and Marshals were prepared to listen to the small, cold bespectacled Major.

And now, just after Ducos's arrival, Marmont's army had been destroyed! It had been humiliated at Salamanca and his so-called Army of Portugal was now running through Spain as fast as it could and even Madrid was being abandoned. Only Soult, Marshal of the Army of the South, was winning victories, but what use were victories over rag-tag Spanish armies when the real war was being fought in Castile?

So Ducos had ridden south, protected from the guerilleros by six hundred cavalrymen, and he had presented Marshal Soult with opportunity, though at first Soult had been unwilling to grasp it. "I cannot spare any men, monsieur," he told Ducos respectfully, mindful that this serpent could hiss in the Emperor's ear. "Wherever you look there are guerilleros! And General Ballesteros's army is intact."

Ballesteros's Spanish army was intact, Ducos thought, because Soult had not destroyed it. He had merely defeated it, and so driven it back to the protection of the great guns of the British garrison at Gibraltar. Defeating Ballesteros was not enough. The enemy had to be annihilated! There was a lack of audacity among the French commanders in Spain, Ducos had decided. They feared losing battles and so did not take the risks which might let them win great victories.

"Ballesteros does not count," Ducos explained patiently, "he is a pawn. The guerilleros do not count. They are merely bandits. Only Wellington's army counts."

"And part of his army is on my northern flank," Soult pointed out. "I have General Hill to my north, Ballesteros to my south, and you want me to send men to help Marmont?"

"No," Ducos said, "I want you to send men to help the Emperor. To help France."

Soult looked at the map. The mention of Napoleon had stilled his protests and in truth the idea that Major Ducos had suggested was not unappealing. It was also daring, very daring. By itself it might not destroy Wellington, but it would certainly throw him off balance and bring him hurrying back to the Portuguese border. Such a retreat would save Madrid, it would give Marmont time to reform his army and it would damage Wellington's reputation. Better still it would add a page of glory to Marshal Soult's long record.

Take a few thousand men, Ducos had suggested, and march them eastwards until they could cross the headwaters of the Guadiana. There they must strike north, through Madridejos to Toledo, where the bridge over the Tagus was still in French hands. The British would find nothing odd in such a manouevre, indeed they would assume that Soult was merely retreating northwards like the rest of the French armies. But from Toledo, Ducos urged, the force should strike north west towards the roads on which Wellington's supply convoys travelled. To reach those vulnerable roads they must cross the barren mountains of the Sierra de Gredos, then bridge the deep, fast-flowing River Tormes. That was the problem, crossing the river, but Ducos had identified a little-used bridge guarded by a mediaeval fortress called San Miguel. At best, Ducos told Soult, San Miguel would be garrisoned by a company of Spaniards, maybe two companies, and once across the bridge the French would be in the flat country across which the British supply lines ran from Portugal. "The British believe they are safe," Ducos urged Soult. "They believe there is not a Frenchman within a hundred miles of those roads! They are sleeping."

And if Soult's picked force could come down from the Sierra de Gredos like a pack of wolves then for a week, no more, they could destroy, capture and kill before they would be forced to march away. A ring of retreating British troops would otherwise tighten about them, but that one week of destruction could save the French in Spain by pulling Wellington back from his pursuit of the beaten Marmont. And such an achievement, Soult told himself again, would make the Emperor very grateful to Nicolas Jean-de Dieu Soult, Duke of

Dalmatia.

So Soult agreed.

And picked six thousand men, of whom a third were cavalry, and put them under the command of his best cavalry general, Jean Herault.

Who now led his men north through Toledo with Ducos by his side. They rode fast, a sleeping enemy ahead, a little and ancient fort their only obstacle and glory in their grasp.

§§§

Major Tubbs insisted that one small room of the fortress, which only had four usable rooms on its three floors, be described as an officer's mess, and there Sharpe, Teresa, Major Tubbs, Lieutenant Price and Ensign Hickey ate. Sharpe, perhaps wanting to unsettle Lucius Tubbs, had insisted on inviting the Major's foreman, Mister MacKeon, and so the Scotsman, who was a tall, frowning man with huge hands, a heavy brow and scowling eyes, sat awkwardly at the makeshift table which, being nothing but an old door stretched across two empty wine barrels was far too small for six people.

Ensign Hickey could not take his eyes from Teresa. He did try once or twice and even ventured a conversation with MacKeon, but MacKeon just scowled at him and Hickey's watery eyes inevitably strayed back to Teresa who was illuminated by the large candles that the village priest had brought from his church. The flamelight cast intriguing shadows on Teresa's face, lit her eyes like stars and Hickey could not help himself. He just gaped at her mournfully.

"You've never seen a woman before, Mister Hickey?" Sharpe snarled.

"Yes, sir. Yes, I have. Yes." Hickey nodded vigorously and pretended to be intent on his cold mutton, beans and rice. He was sixteen, new to the battalion and in awe of Captain Sharpe. "I'm sorry, sir," he mumbled, reddening.

"Don't apologise, Hickey," Harry Price said, "just stare away, dear boy, stare away! I do! I like staring at Mrs Sharpe. She's a damned watchable lady if you'll forgive me saying so, Ma'am."

"I forgive you, Harry." Teresa said.

"You're the first woman who ever has forgiven him," Sharpe said to his wife.

"Not fair, Richard," Price said, "I'm forever being forgiven by women."

Hickey was again gazing at Teresa and, realising that Sharpe was looking at him, he tried to make conversation. "You really do fight, Ma'am?"

"When I have to," Teresa said, breaking a loaf of bread apart.

"Against the French, Ma'am?" Hickey enquired.

"Who the hell else?" Sharpe growled.

"Against all men who are rude," Teresa said, dazzling Hickey with a smile, "but I have fought the French, Mister Hickey, since the day they killed my family."

"Oh, my Lord," Hickey said. Such things did not happen in Danbury, Essex, where his family farmed three hundred placid acres.

"And I am at San Miguel to fight them again," Teresa said.

"No French here, Ma'am," Major Tubbs said happily. "Not a frog within hopping distance." He smiled, delighted with his small jest. "Not in hopping distance, eh?"

"And if one does come within hopping distance," Teresa explained to the dazzled Ensign Hickey, "then my men will see them coming. We are your cavalry scouts."

"And glad we are to have you, Ma'am," Tubbs said gallantly.

John MacKeon, who until now had stayed silent, suddenly looked at Sharpe and the fierceness of the Scotsman's gaze was so intense that it brought an awkward silence to the cramped table. "You no remember me?" He said to Sharpe.

Sharpe looked at the craggy face with its thick eyebrows and deep-set eyes. "Should I, Mister MacKeon?"

"I was with you, Sharpe, when you crossed the wall at Gawilghur."

"Then I should remember you," Sharpe said.

"Ah, no," MacKeon said dismissively. "I was just another soldier. One of Campbell's men in the 96th, ye remember them?"

Sharpe nodded. "I remember them. I remember Captain Campbell too."

"Now there's a laddie who's done well for himself," MacKeon said, "and no more than he's deserved, I dare say. It was a great day's work ye both did."

"We all did it," Sharpe said.

"But you were first across the wall, man. I remember seeing you climb and I thought to myself, there's a dead man if ever I did see one!"

"What happened?" Teresa asked.

Sharpe shrugged. "It was in India. A battle. We won."

Teresa raised her eyebrows in mock surprise. "What a wonderful story teller you are, Richard. A battle. In India. We won."

"Aye," MacKeon said, shaking his head. "Gawilghur! A rare fight, that one. A rare fight. A horde of heathen, there were, a horde! And the horde were mewed up tight in a great fort, big as heaven it was, with walls to the sky. And this wee laddie," he gestured at Sharpe, "scrambled up the cliff like a monkey. A dead man if ever I did see one. Aye," he nodded at Sharpe, "I thought it was you."

"So what did happen?" Tubbs demanded, echoing Teresa's earlier plea.

"It was a battle," Sharpe said, getting to his feet, "in India."

"And you won?" Teresa asked earnestly, making Harry Price smile.

"We did," Sharpe said, "we did." He paused, thinking, and it almost seemed he was going to tell the story, but instead he touched a finger to the long scar that ran up one cheek and which gave him such a grim appearance. "I fetched this scar in that fight," he said, then shook his head, "but if you'll forgive me, it's time to check the sentries." He picked up his shako, rifle and sword belt and ducked out the door.

"It was a battle," Teresa said, imitating Sharpe, "in India. We won. So what really happened, Mister MacKeon?"

"He just told you, didn't he?" The Scotsman demanded. "It was a battle in India, and we won it." McKeon scowled and lapsed into his previous silence.

Sharpe crossed the bridge, spoke to the two men who stood guard at the southern end, then went back to the picquets at the northern side, and afterwards he climbed the wooden ladders in the fortress, past the room where Hickey still stared forlornly at Teresa, and found Patrick Harper on the southern parapet. The Sergeant's seven barrel gun, a monstrous weapon made for the navy which bundled seven half inch barrels onto one stock, was propped in a corner of the battlement, while Harper's rifle was on his shoulder. He nodded a greeting to Sharpe, then offered his canteen.

Sharpe shook his head. "I'm not thirsty, Pat."

"That's medicine in there, so it is," Harper said, "and it's not the sort of medicine that cures disease, sir. Medicine for the soul."

"Ah," Sharpe took the canteen and drank some of the red wine. "So how many bottles did you keep back?"

"None that I know of, sir," Harper said in a voice of injured innocence, "but I might have missed a few. It's dark in that store-room, so it is, especially when the door's shut, and it's easy to miss a few dark bottles in a black place." He drank from the canteen. "But the boys got your message, Mister Sharpe, so they did, and they know that if one of them gets drunk I'll kill him myself."

"And keep Mister Price away from the bottles," Sharpe said. Lieutenant Price was a good companion, but much too fond of liquor.

"I'll do my best, so I will," Harper promised, then stared south down the long white road that finally vanished among the distant hills. There was a half moon in the western sky and the olive groves, which filled the landscape to the west, looked silvered and calm. Bats constantly flew from the vast cracks and gaping holes in the fort's tired masonry. Sharpe went to the western parapet and gazed at the village where a handful of lights showed, then he leaned over to look down into the vineyard which grew close up against the fort's wall. Nothing stirred in the night except the bats and the clouds flying glitter-edged towards the moon and the river sliding endlessly on its long journey that looped about the plain where Marshal Marmont had been thrashed by Wellington. "Are we expecting trouble here?" Harper asked.

"No, Pat," Sharpe said. "Soft duty."

"Soft duty, eh? Then why give it to you?"

"I'm still recovering from the wound." Sharpe said, patting his belly where a Frenchman's pistol bullet had injured him.

"So it's a convalescent you are, eh?" Harper chuckled. "Good job there's still some medicine about the place then, eh?"

"A good job, Pat," Sharpe said softly, then fingered the ancient parapet and wondered how old the fortress was. Five hundred years? Probably more. It was in dreadful condition, nothing more than a square stone shell of weathered walls that were thick with weeds and so riven with cracks that it looked as if one good kick would bring the old masonry tumbling down. The fort must have been abandoned years ago, but the present war had revived its usefulness as a look-out post and so the Spanish, and after them the French, had rebuilt its collapsed floors in timber and put a staircase of wooden ladders up to the western parapet. An original stone stairway still ran down to the courtyard from the eastern rampart where an archway, missing its gates, opened onto the bridge's approach road. The store-room where the wine and muskets had been found occupied the whole western side of the fort and was the only stone chamber left in San Miguel. The room had an elegant curved ceiling and Sharpe guessed the room might once have been a chapel, but then, after the rest of the fort's interior had collapsed, someone had driven a door through the outer northern wall so the space could be used as a cattle byre. Now, for a time at least, the ruined fort had been restored to martial duty, though it had precious little value except as an observation post for the old stones would not last five minutes against a cannonade.

Sharpe stared at the moonlit fields across the river. There was a farm just two hundred yards down the road, a small place with a white-walled yard and a tower above the entrance gate. A good place for a battery of cannon, he thought, because the artillerymen could knock loopholes in the farmyard wall and so be safe from rifle fire and the Frogs would have the fort of San Miguel reduced to dust and rubble in less time than it would take to soft boil an egg, and then their infantry would come from the olive groves on the other side of the road, and how the hell would he defend San Miguel then? But there would be no attack, he told himself, and even if there were, the partisans in the Sierra de Gredos would send warning of the French approach and Sharpe would have a full day in which to summon reinforcements from Salamanca.

But that would not happen. He was only supposed to stay here one week, after which a Spanish garrison would arrive. One week for Tubbs to sort through the captured muskets, and that week should be uneventful. A rest. "I don't know why they bother to send a full Commissary Officer to do this work," Sharpe said, staring down into the courtyard where Tubbs's ox-wagon waited for the muskets.

"I don't think 'they' sent him," Harper said, "he sent himself, sir, if you follow my meaning."

24

"Which I don't."

Harper held out a huge right hand and rocked it to and fro. "There's five thousand muskets, sir, near enough, and who's to say how many Mister Tubbs will condemn? And who's to know when he sells the condemned ones? There's a pretty penny to be made out of those guns, so there is."

"He's on the take?"

"Who isn't?" Harper asked, "and Mister MacKeon reckons Tubbs will condemn at least half of them, and if they only fetched a shilling apiece that'd be a fair profit."

"I should have known the bastard was on the fiddle," Sharpe growled.

"How were you to know?" Harper asked. "I wouldn't have guessed if Mister MacKeon hadn't told me. He's an interesting fellow. You know he was once a swoddy? In the 96th, he was. He reckons he saw you in India."

"So he says."

"And he says you took a fortress all by yourself?"

"And I killed a giant," Sharpe said, "just before I jumped over the moon."

"And he says you should tell me the story."

Sharpe grimaced. "That's just what you need, Pat, another bloody war story. What time are you being relieved?"

"Two in the morning, sir." Harper said, then watched as Sharpe turned and went down the ladders. "And good night to you too, sir," he said, and just then Sharpe turned and climbed back up again.

Sharpe stood on the rampart, gazing at emptiness, and the half moon touched a shadow from the scar on his face. He stood a long time, his left hand gripping the hilt of his brutal great sword. "I don't like it, Pat," he said after the stretching silence.

"Don't like what, sir?"

"This." Sharpe crossed to the parapet and frowned southwards. "I just don't like it."

Harper shrugged. "The Crapauds can't come from Salamanca, sir, because it's in our hands, so it is, and they can't come through those big hills," he pointed south, "because they're full of guerilleros, and that means they can't come at all, sir." He paused, waiting for Sharpe's reaction, but none came. "Unless they fly here, sir, they won't be coming."

Sharpe nodded. Everything the big Irish sergeant said made sense, but Sharpe could not shake his unease. "There was a fellow called Manu Bappoo in India, Pat."

"Mannie who, sir?"

"Manu Bappoo," Sharpe repeated the name, "and he was a good soldier. Better than most of them, but we still beat the bugger somewhere or other, can't remember the name of the place, and Bappoo went running back to Gawilghur. It was a fortress, see? Great big place it was, not like this. And high up, high in the bloody sky, and Manu Bappoo reckoned he was safe there. He reckoned he couldn't be beaten up there, Pat, because no one had ever taken that fortress and no one believed it could be took." Sharpe paused, remembering Gawilghur's dark walls and the sheer cliffs that protected them. Hell in a high place. "He was over-confident, see? Just like us here."

"So what happened?" Harper asked.

"Some daft bugger in a red coat climbed a cliff," Sharpe said, "and that was the end of Manu Bappoo."

"No cliffs here, sir."

"But keep your eyes peeled. I just don't like it."

"Goodnight, Mister Sharpe," Harper said when Sharpe had disappeared a second time down the makeshift staircase. Then the Irishman turned back to the south where nothing moved, except a falling star that blazed briefly in the sky above the Sierra and then was gone.

He's got the shakes, Harper thought. He's seeing enemies where there are none. But the Irishman kept his eyes peeled anyway.

§§§

General Jean Herault was just thirty years old. He was a cavalryman, an hussar, and he wore the cadenettes of the hussars; the twin pigtails that framed his face and were the distinctive marks of the hussars. His jacket was a waist-length, skin-tight dolman, a Hungarian fashion because hussar was a Hungarian word, and Herault's dolman was brown with pale blue cuffs and bright with thick white loops of lace sewn across its breast. His breeches were pale blue and had still more lace twisting and looping down the thighs

26

towards the tasselled tops of his black leather boots. The general had once been the captain of an elite company and he still wore their mark; the thick fur colback hat with its tall red plume. The colback was hot in summer, but it stopped a sabre slash better than any metal helmet. From his left shoulder hung a fur-trimmed pelisse that was even more thickly decorated with white lace than his coat, while a blue and white sash crossed his chest and a white leather belt held the silver chains from which his sabre scabbard hung. A sabretache, decorated with the eagle of France, hung by the scabbard. The sabre was curved, sharp as a witch's tongue and, in Herault's hand, lethal.

A very handsome man, Jean Herault, and made even more handsome by his gorgeous uniform. There were girls across Europe who sighed at the memory of Herault, the slim light-horseman who had ridden into town, broken their hearts and ridden away, but Herault was much more than a handsome young killer on a horse. He was also clever. And he was lucky. And he was brave.

Herault had led a charge at Albuhera that had destroyed a British battalion and even though that battle had been lost, Herault had emerged covered in glory. It was a glory that had been enhanced in the battles against Ballesteros's Spaniards, and Soult had promoted the young cavalry officer to command all the Army of the South's horsemen, and Herault had led them brilliantly. He had done the dull work well, and that was an even more impressive achievement than doing the brave work gloriously. Any fool could be a hero if he had luck and daring enough, but it took a clever man to do war's day-to-day chores well, and Herault's cavalry patrolled and scouted and manned an outpost line that was forever under assault by partisans, and Herault had made sure they did it aggressively and efficiently. He had even persuaded his men not to treat every Spanish peasant as an enemy, for doing so only made them into enemies, and for the first time in Spain Soult was beginning to receive information from civilians, information that was freely given instead of extracted by torture. Herault had achieved that.

Now Herault had to capture the bridge at San Miguel de Tormes, and even before he left Toledo he had given the problem a good deal of thought. He had even managed to impress Pierre Ducos and that was quite an achievement, for Ducos believed most soldiers were pig-headed fools. "The danger," Herault explained to the Major who was not really a Major, "is going through the mountains."

"Because of the guerilleros?" Ducos asked, "so travel at night."

"But however fast we travel, Major, the guerilleros will still out-run us and so give warning to this fortlet at San Miguel," Herault tapped the map, "and the fort's garrison will send to Salamanca for reinforcements and we shall arrive and find a small army waiting for us." He frowned, staring at the map and tapping his teeth with a pencil. "Avila," he said after a while, prodding the town with the pencil. It lay well to the east of San Miguel, high in the hills.

"Avila?" Ducos asked.

"If I march towards Avila it will draw the guerilleros like flies to a corpse. And I shall send a vanguard, say three hundred infantry? We give the bastards a victory, Major, by sacrificing those three hun-dred men on the Avila road, and when the guerilleros are busy destroying them, the rest of us will go straight across the hills." He slashed the pencil across the map. "My two thousand cavalrymen will go first, and we shall ride like demons, Major. Any horse that falls will be left, its rider abandoned. We will ride straight for San Miguel, and you will follow with the infantry. It will take the foot-soldiers two days, less if General Michaud forces them hard, and we shall hold the bridge at San Miguel until you come."

Michaud would force the infantry hard. Ducos would see to that, using all the Emperor's surrogate authority to make Michaud crack the whip. "But what about the British reinforcements from Salamanca?" Ducos asked. "Suppose they arrive before Michaud?"

"They won't know where to go, Major," Herault said, "because I won't just wait for Michaud to catch up. I shall send cavalry all across the plain, right to the gates of Ciudad Rodrigo. We shall burn supplies, ambush convoys and kill every small garrison. We shall set southern Castile afire, Major, and the British will march in circles try-ing to find us." He let the map roll up.

"And what does the infantry do?"

"It stays at San Miguel, of course. To protect our retreat."

Ducos approved. Madrid would be saved, Marmont's retreat could end, and the British would be forced back to the Portuguese border to protect their supply route, only to discover that their enemy had vanished into the hills. It was an audacious plan, brilliant even, and proof to Ducos that a few brave men could change the course of a war. Herault, he thought, must be recommended to the Emperor, and he wrote the general's name in his small black notebook and added a star which was Ducos's code for a man who might well deserve swift promotion.

"We leave at dawn," Herault said, then smiled, "and tonight my men will spread rumours that we intend to sack Avila. By tomorrow night, Major, every partisan within fifty miles will be waiting on the Avila road."

And Herault would be miles away, spurring towards a fortress that thought itself safe.

§§§

It was uncanny how news spread in the Spanish countryside. Other than a few old men who tended the oxen turning the wheels that pumped the river water into the irrigation ditches Sharpe could see no one in the fields, olive groves and vineyards across the river, but by midday a rumour had reached Teresa's partisans that a French column had marched from Toledo to sack Avila. The rumour enraged Teresa. "It is a special place!" she claimed.

"Avila?" Sharpe asked, "special?"

"Saint Teresa lived there."

"Must be special then." Sharpe said sarcastically.

Teresa bridled at his tone. "What would you know about it? Protestant pig."

"I'm not any sort of pig. Not protestant, not nothing."

"Heathen pig, then," Teresa said angrily. She stared eastwards. "I should ride there," she added.

"I won't stop you," Sharpe said, "but I won't be happy."

"Who cares about your happiness?"

"Your men are my best sentries." Sharpe said. "If anything does come up that road," he pointed southwards, "your men will see it first." Teresa's partisans were keeping watch in the foothills, ready to ride back and warn San Miguel of any threat coming out of the Sierra de Gredos. "How far is Avila, anyway?"

Teresa shrugged. "Fifty miles."

"And why would the frogs go there?"

"For plunder, of course!" Teresa said. "There are rich convents, monasteries, the cathedral, the basilica of Santa Vicente."

"But why would they go after plunder?" Sharpe asked.

Teresa frowned at him, wondering why he asked such a seeming-ly stupid question. "Because they are Crapauds, of course!" she final-ly answered. "Because they are scum. Because they are slime-toads that dropped from the devil's backside when God was not watching."

"But everywhere else," Sharpe said, "the church treasures are hid-den." Sharpe had marched through countless Spanish towns and vil-lages, and everywhere the church plate had been taken away and buried or else concealed behind walls or hidden in caves. He had seen precious altar screens, too large to be moved, daubed with lime-wash in hope that the French would not realise there was treasure behind the white covering. What he had never seen was a church flaunting its treasures when the French were within a week's march. "Why would Avila keep its treasures?"

"How would I know?" Teresa responded indignantly.

"And the frogs know damn well that church treasures are hidden," Sharpe said, "so why are they going there?"

"You tell me," Teresa said.

"Because they want you to think they're going there," he said, "that's why. And all the time the bastards are going somewhere else. God damn it!" He turned around again to stare south. Was it just nerves? Was he frightened of this small responsibility? Was he not fit to guard a derelict fort in a backwater of the war? Or was his instinct, that had served him so well through over fifteen years of fighting, telling him to be careful? "Keep your men here, love," he said to Teresa, "because I think you're going to have frogs to kill." He turned and ran towards the parapet that looked down onto the bridge and he leaned far out to shout down at the roadway. "Sergeant Harper!"

Harper emerged from the shrine built on the far verge and blinked up at Sharpe who, leaning over the fort parapet, was silhouetted against the sky. "Sir?"

"My compliments to Major Tubbs, Sergeant, and I want his ox-cart on the bridge. As a barricade, got it? And I want you and twen-ty Riflemen up at that damn farm," he pointed southwards across the river, "and I want it all done now!"

Teresa put a hand on his green sleeve. "You really think the

French are coming here, Richard?"

"I don't think it, I know it! I know it! I don't know how I know it, but I do. The buggers have slipped round the side gate and are coming in through the back door."

Major Tubbs, sweating in the day's heat, came lumbering up the stone stairway from the courtyard. "You can't block the bridge, Captain Sharpe!" Tubbs protested. "You can't! It's a public thoroughfare."

"If I had the powder, Major, I'd blow the bloody bridge up."

Tubbs looked into Sharpe's grim face, then gazed southwards. "But the French aren't coming! Look!"

Sharpe looked and the southern landscape was wonderfully peaceful. Poppies fluttered in the breeze that rippled the crops and flickered the pale leaves of the olive groves. There was no smoke rising from burning villages to smear the sky, and no plume of dust kicked up by thousands of boots and hooves. There was just a peaceful summer landscape, basking in Castilian heat. God was in his heaven and all was well in the world. "But they're coming," Sharpe said obstinately.

"Then why don't we warn Salamanca?" Tubbs asked.

That was a good question, a damned good question, but Sharpe did not want to articulate his answer. He knew he should warn Salamanca, but he was scared of raising a false alarm. It was only his instinct that contradicted the peaceful appearance of the landscape, and what if he were wrong? Suppose that the garrison at Salamanca marched out half a battalion of redcoats and a battery of field guns, and with them a supply convoy and a squadron of dragoons, and all of it proved a waste? What would they say then? That Captain Sharpe, up from the ranks, was an alarmist. That he couldn't be trusted with responsibility. That he might be useful enough in a tight corner when there were frogs to be killed, but he was nervous as a virgin in a barrack's town when left to himself. "We don't warn Salamanca," he told Tubbs firmly, "because we can deal with the bastards ourselves."

"You can?" Tubbs asked dubiously.

"Have you ever fought a battle, Major?" Sharpe turned angrily on Tubbs.

"My dear fellow, I wasn't doubting you!" Tubbs held up both

31

hands as though to ward Sharpe off. "My own nerves giving tongue, nothing more. Tremulous, they are. I ain't a soldier like you. Of course you're right!"

Sharpe hoped to God he was, but he knew he was not. He knew he should summon reinforcements, but he feared what men would say if those reinforcements were not needed and so he would stay and fight alone because he was too proud to lose face by appearing to be nervous. "We'll beat the bastards," he said, "if they come."

"I'm sure they won't," Tubbs said.

And Sharpe prayed that Tubbs was right.

§§§

Three hundred French infantrymen were sacrificed in the defiles of the road that led up to Avila, and from all across the Sierra de Gredos partisans flooded to the fight, hurrying over the hills for this chance to slaughter the hated enemy. The three hundred men seemed to have marched too far ahead of the rest of their column, and they were doomed, for the other Frenchmen did not hurry to their assistance, but made camp in the plain. And there were too many Frenchmen camped on that southern plain, so the partisans concentrated on the doomed three hundred infantrymen who had ventured a march too far into the hills.

And when night fell, and when the sound of the slaughter still sounded from the Avila road, Herault marched.

He took all his cavalry due west across the plain and, when he had gone some five miles and the sound of the distant musketry was almost inaudible, he turned north onto a track that led across the lower hills of the western sierra. He led hussars, dragoons and lancers, men who had fought all across Europe, men who were feared all across Europe, but Herault knew that the great days of the French cavalry were passing. It was not their bravery that had diminished, but their horses. The animals were weak from poor food, their backs were ulcerated from too much riding and so, gradually but inevitably, Herault's column stretched. There were no guerilleros to slow them, it was the horses that could not keep up, and Herault, who was well mounted himself, paused at one hill crest and looked back in the thin moonlight to see his men faltering. He had planned to be at San

Miguel at dawn, when the garrison's spirits would be at their lowest and he had imagined bursting from the hills in a monstrous display of steel and uniformed glory, but he now knew that his two thousand men would never reach the river in time. Their horses would not make it. A few beasts had gone lame, others breathed with a hollow whistling, and most hung their weary heads low.

But what two thousand men could not do, one hundred might, and Herault's old elite company of hussars, the men with the black fur colbacks, were mounted on the best horses Herault had been able to find. He had pampered that troop, not just because it was his old company, but because he always needed at least one squadron of cavalry that was mounted as well as any enemy horsemen. And he had foreseen this crisis. He had hoped it would not happen, he had hoped that a miracle might take place and that his two thousand horses would all have the stamina of Bucephalus, but that miracle had not happened and so it was time for the elite hussars to ride ahead.

Herault summoned the commander of the elite company to his side and gestured back down the struggling column. "You see what's happening?"

Captain Michel Pailleterie, his blond pigtails and moustache looking almost white in the moonlight, nodded. "I see, my General, yes."

"So you know what to do."

Pailleterie drew his sabre and saluted Herault. "When can we expect you, my general?"

"Midday."

"I shall have a hot meal ready," Pailleterie said with a smile.

Herault leaned across and embraced the Captain who was only a year younger than himself. "*Bonne chance, mon brave!*"

"Who needs luck against a company of dozy Spaniards, eh?" Pailleterie asked, and then he pointed his sabre forward and the elite company rode on alone. And God help them, Herault thought, if any partisans still lingered on the road. "I wish I was going with you," he called after the company, but they had already vanished. The best of the best, Herault's elite, was riding to snatch victory. "Onwards!" Herault ordered the rest of the cavalry, "onwards!"

The lucky ones of the three hundred infantrymen had either escaped out of the hills or else were dead. The unlucky had been captured. Some of those prisoners would be roasted over slow fires, some would be skinned alive, others would suffer still worse, and the only mercy for them was that, eventually, they would all die. Herault regretted their fate, but they had served their purpose, for his cavalry was loose in the hills and the partisans were far away.

And the remaining French infantry, all three thousand seven hundred of them, were following fast. The ruse had worked, the guerilleros had been lured out of the way and the back door of Castile lay open.

§§§

The moon touched the walls of the farmhouse beyond the river a ghostly white. Sharpe had twenty riflemen behind those walls, put there to hold up any French advance down the road. The riflemen could probably stop an attacking column for ten minutes and after that Harper would have to bring them running back to the river where the rest of Sharpe's riflemen and all his redcoats were posted. The riflemen were on the fort's parapet while Lieutenant Price had the redcoats lined behind the cart which served as a barricade. Sharpe had been tempted to add to the barricade by taking carts and furniture from the villagers, but he had resisted the temptation. The villagers had suffered enough from the war, and they had been welcoming his men by shyly bringing them gifts of olives, eggs and freshly caught fish. The single cart would have to suffice.

"But why would the French come here?" Teresa asked. They were standing on the fort's parapet.

"If they can retake Salamanca," Sharpe said, "they cut Wellington off from his supplies. They don't even need to take the city to do that! Just sit on the road to Ciudad Rodrigo. In a couple of days the supplies will dry up, and Nosey will have to turn round and come back to deal with the buggers. He won't be best pleased."

"So we must stop them?"

Sharpe nodded.

"So why don't you send for reinforcements?"

Sharpe shrugged.

"Because you're not sure they're coming?" Teresa asked.

"I can't be sure," he said.

"And you're frightened of looking like a fool?"

"If I raise an alarm," Sharpe said, "and no crapauds come, they'll string my guts out and hang their washing out to dry on them. I'll be a quartermaster for the rest of my days! They'll never trust me again."

Teresa shook her head. "Richard, you took a French eagle! You crossed the breach at Badajoz! You have pride to spare!" Her eyes blazed in the moonlight, but Sharpe said nothing. "So write a request now," she added.

"You don't understand," he said softly. "I could snatch a thousand French eagles and I'm still the bugger who came up from the ranks. I'm still an upstart. They can smell me a hundred yards off, and they're just waiting, Teresa, just waiting for me to make a mistake. Just one mistake. That's all it takes."

"Write a request now," she said patiently, "and as soon as the first Frenchman shows, I will ride to Salamanca. As soon as we hear the first gunshot in the hills, I will ride. So then you will not have to hold for long, Richard."

He thought about it and knew she was right, and so he went down to the mess and lit a candle and then woke Ensign Hickey because the Ensign had gone to a proper school and had respectable hand-writing, while Sharpe's penmanship was crude and almost illegible, and once Hickey was awake Sharpe dictated the message that was addressed to the officer commanding the British and allied forces in Salamanca. "I have reason to believe," he spoke slowly, "that a French column is approaching this fort which I have the honour to command." He paused, thinking. What reason did he have to believe in a French attack? No reason but instinct. He was like the lad in the schoolroom story who cried wolf, but the letter was not to be sent, just to be written in case his instinct turned out to be sound. Hickey, worried by Sharpe's long pause, was gazing up at him, wide-eyed, the candle guttering and smoky on the table. "My command being perilously small in numbers," Sharpe continued, "I request that reinforcements may be sent as quickly as may be possible. Richard Sharpe, Capt'. Shouldn't I date it?" he asked Teresa, "put a time on it?"

"I will convince them you were in a hurry," Teresa said.

Hickey, shy to be seen in front of Teresa in his undershirt, pulled a blanket over his bare legs, then blew on the ink to dry it. "Are the French really coming, sir?" He asked Sharpe.

"I reckon so. Why? Does that worry you?"

Hickey thought about it for a heartbeat, then nodded. "Yes, sir, it does,"

"It's why you joined the army, isn't it?" Sharpe demanded harshly.

"I joined the army, sir, because my father wanted me to."

"He wanted you dead?"

"I pray not, sir." Hickey said humbly. Teresa stood by the door, wondering why her husband was so hard on the boy.

"I was an Ensign once, Hickey," Sharpe said, leaning down and adding his signature to the letter, "and I learned one lesson about being an Ensign."

"And what lesson was that, sir?"

"That ensigns are expendable, Hickey, expendable. Now go back to sleep."

Sharpe and Teresa climbed back to the parapet. "You were cruel, Richard," she said.

"I was honest."

"You think he will be a better soldier because he is frightened of you?"

"I think he'll be a better soldier if he learns to cope with fear," Sharpe growled.

Teresa thought about that, then shrugged. "And were you expendable?" she asked, "as an ensign?"

"I climbed a cliff, love. That's what I did as an Ensign, I climbed a cliff. And they reckoned I would die, and none would have cared much if I had."

And who would be climbing the cliff in the morning, he wondered. And where? And how? And what had he forgotten? And would the bastards come? And could he stop them? And Jesus, he was nervous. He had listened to his instinct, and he was ready for the French, but it still felt all wrong. It felt like defeat, and it had not even started yet.

§§§

Teresa's men, three miles south of San Miguel in the foothills of the Sierra de Gredos, roasted a brace of hares over an open fire. They

36

lit the fire in a grove of trees, deep in a rocky cleft, and they were sure that the fire's light could not be seen on the road which lay white beneath their position. If one Frenchman dared breathe on that road the partisans would fire their muskets and so warn the fort that the enemy was coming.

But Captain Pailleterie saw a gleam of their fire. It was a tiny gleam, merely a reflection of a leaping flame on a high rock, but he knew only two kinds of men had fires in the hills; partisans or soldiers, and both kind were his enemies. He held up his hand and checked the company.

The gleam had been to the left of the high track, at least he thought so, for he was still not in sight of the stretch of road that ran directly beneath the rocky bluff where he had seen the faint glimmer. Off to his right there was a dark valley and it seemed to him that it curled around to the north and so might offer a way to the river and to the bridge which would be hidden from whoever had carelessly lit a fire in this dark night.

His men all had muffled scabbards so that the metal did not clash against a buckle or a stirrup. Pailleterie could do little about the sound of their hooves, so that was a risk that must be taken. "We go slowly now," he told his men, "slow and quiet."

They swerved off to the right, walking their tired horses through the gentle grassy valley that did indeed turn to the north. Then the land rose to a crest and Pailleterie sweated as he led the hundred horsemen up to that skyline for the saddle of moonlit land was scattered with grey rocks that could hide a hundred partisans and it would be a perfect place for an ambush, but no musket fired.

He curbed his horse just south of the crest, gave its reins to a sergeant, then dismounted and walked uphill until he could just see over the hill's top.

Peace. That was all he could see, peace. A wide, moonlit land, though the moon was paling now as dawn came around the world, and in the grey white light of night's ending he could see the sheen of a river, and black trees, and then the white streak of the road and the black square shape of the old fort. No fires there, and for a moment Pailleterie dared to hope that San Miguel would be unguarded, but he put that hope aside as he moved forward another few paces and realised there was a god after all. There was a god, and He was a

Frenchman, for a spur of hill jutted out to hide his men all the way from the crest down to the plain, and once on the plain they would be hidden from San Miguel's garrison by the olive groves. He edged back from the crest, straightened and walked down his column. "Load your pistols now, but don't cock them. You hear me? Load, but don't cock them. If anyone fires before we reach the bridge I will personally drown that man! But I will geld him first!" He watched as his men loaded their long-barrelled pistols. The weapons were not accurate, but at close quarters they were as deadly as any musket. "We shall ride slowly down the hill. Very slowly! We shall move as quietly as a man coming to his married lover at midnight. We shall glide like a morning mist, and then we shall stay among the trees. We will go slowly, you hear me? And none of you will sneeze! If you sneeze, I will geld you with a blunt knife. And we do not charge till the last minute, and when we reach the bridge you will kill whoever you find there. Kill and kill! And if you fail? I shall geld you with my own teeth. With my own blunt teeth!"

The hussars grinned. They liked Pailleterie, for he looked after them, he was brave and he gave them victory.

And he was about to give them another.

§§§

It was almost dawn, no warning shots had been fired from the hills and Sharpe felt an immense weariness. He felt foolish, too. There were no French coming. It had been nerves, he thought. Nerves as tight as a snare drum, and what kind of a soldier got nervous? Damn it, he thought, but maybe he could not be trusted with command. Maybe the bullet he had received at the battle inside Salamanca had done more than wound him, perhaps it had made him fearful.

He walked to the western side of the fort's parapet and leaned over to stare down at the barricade on the bridge. He had all his men awake, all on guard, for it was coming up to dawn and that was the most dangerous time. "Are you alert down there?" He shouted.

"Bright as buttercups, sir," Lieutenant Price answered. "Can you see anything, sir?"

"Bugger all, Harry."

"That's a relief, sir."

Sharpe went back to the northern parapet and gazed over the vine-yard at the Salamanca road. Nothing moved there. Quiet as the damn grave. A few last bats still flew around the tower, and earlier he had seen an owl come flapping in to a hole in the fort's decaying stonework, but otherwise it was still. He went back to the southern wall above the river that slid silent beneath a smoke-like layer of mist. The bridge's three arches were dark. Sergeant Harper reckoned he had seen some large trout in the sinuous weeds beneath those arch-es, but Sharpe had given him no time to try and catch them. It was nerves, he thought again. He was jumpy as hell, and he had made everyone else nervous.

Teresa came up the ladder stairs from the living quarters. She yawned, then put her arm into Sharpe's elbow and rested her head on his shoulder. "All quiet?"

"All quiet." There were four riflemen up on the parapet. Sharpe had thought to put some redcoats up here, but their smoothbore mus-kets were so inaccurate that they could do little good from this height and so he had merely kept his remaining riflemen here. He moved away from them so they would not overhear him. "I'm thinking I panicked yesterday," he said to Teresa.

"I didn't see you panic."

"Seeing enemies where there aren't any," he admitted.

She squeezed his arm. "At least you are ready for them if they come."

He grimaced. "But they're not out there, are they? They're bloody miles away, tucked up in their beds and I've had a sleepless night because of it."

"You can sleep today," Teresa said. The eastern sky was ablaze now, banded with clouds that reflected the first sunlight . The olive groves, still in night's shadows, were dark, but in another few minutes the sun would rise over the hills and Sharpe would stand the compa-ny down. Give them an easy day, he thought, for they deserved it. A make and mend day in which they could sew up their uniforms, or just sleep, or perhaps fish in the river or go to the village and stare at the girls.

"Perhaps I will go back to Salamanca today," Teresa said.

"Leaving me?"

"Just for the day," she said, "to visit Antonia."

Antonia was their daughter, a baby, but she might as well have been an orphan, Sharpe reckoned, for her parents were both so busy killing frogs. "If the weather stays nice," he said, "and the frogs don't come, you could bring her out here?"

"Why not?" Teresa agreed.

"A week here will be good for her," Sharpe said, thinking how his men would spoil the baby outrageously.

"I shall bring her," Teresa said. The sun slipped above the hills and Sharpe flinched from its dazzling light. The shadows of trees and hedgerows stretched long across the road where no Frenchmen stirred. Mister MacKeon strolled from the fort and went to the river-bank where he unbuttoned his trousers and pissed into the Tormes. "Turning wine into water," Teresa said softly.

Then there was a shout from the bridge, and Sharpe turned, and he heard the hooves and he was unslinging his rifle, but he could not see a damn thing because the sun was so low and it was filling the eastern sky with a dazzling light, but coming from the heart of the blinding glare were horsemen.

Not from the road, but from the east, from among the gnarled olive trees that had hidden them, and Sharpe shouted a warning, but it was already too late. "Mister Price!"

"Sir!"

"Let them get close!"

But Price misheard, or else panicked, and shouted at the redcoats to fire and the muskets flamed towards the olive groves, but at much too long a range. Then the first rifles fired from the parapet, jetting smoke a dozen feet from the stonework. Mister MacKeon, still unbuttoned, had seized a musket and blasted it across the river. Sharpe unslung his rifle, aimed at a horseman close to the bank, pulled the trigger and his target was immediately hidden by smoke as the rifle's brass butt hammered back into his shoulder. "Teresa," he shouted, "Teresa!" but Teresa was already running down the court-yard stairs to fetch her horse. Sharpe began to reload the rifle and heard the sound of hooves on the bridge's stone. Christ, he thought, I'm in the wrong place. Can't do a damn thing up here! "Daniel!" he shouted at Hagman, the senior rifleman on the parapet.

"Sir?" Hagman was ramming his rifle.

"I'm going down! Don't get trapped up here!"

"We'll be all right, sir," Hagman said stoically. The old poacher had a face like a grave-digger, hair down to his shoulder blades and was the best man Sharpe and Harper had.

Sharpe took the stairs four at a time. He had been right all along, but he had also been wrong. He had expected the damned French to come straight down the road, straight into his rifles like lambs to the slaughter, and the buggers had fooled him. The buggers had fooled him! They had come down the far river bank, hidden by the rising sun, and now they were on the bridge. Teresa, up in the saddle of her white-eyed and excited horse, waved the letter to him as an explanation of where she was going, then she spurred out through the open arch and turned her horse towards Salamanca.

Muskets banged on the bridge, then other guns sounded. Pistols, Sharpe thought as he recognised the crisper tone of the smaller weapons. A man screamed. Other men were shouting. Sharpe landed heavily at the foot of the stairs and ran through the arch.

And saw instantly that the fort was lost. He had failed.

§§§

Captain Pailleterie had not even reckoned on the sun's help, but the God of War boasted a Frenchman's blue coat that morning and just before the hussar captain released his men from the concealment of the olive trees the sun slid across the horizon to slash its blinding light into the defenders' faces.

"Charge!" Pailleterie shouted, and rowelled back his spurs to drive his big black horse straight for the bridge that was now less than a quarter mile away. One last effort from the horse, that was all he wanted, and he spurred her again and saw puffs of smoke appear at the fort's high parapet, then more smoke showed at the bridge. Bullets flecked the turf, hitting no one. A wagon made a crude barricade on the bridge itself. Behind the wagon were redcoats. British! Not Spanish, but Pailleterie did not care. They were all enemies of France, all better dead. "Charge!" He drew the word out, using it as a war cry, and a flickering thought went through his mind that there was nothing in the world, not even a woman, who could give a joy like this. A horse at full gallop, an enemy surprised, a sabre drawn and death in your grip.

More smoke, this time from the left, from a farmhouse, and Pailleterie was dimly aware of one of his troopers tumbling, of a horse screaming and a sabre skidding along the ground, but then he swerved into the lingering smoke that hung above the bridge's roadway and swung out of the saddle even before his horse had come to a halt. A single musket banged, spewing stinging smoke into Pailleterie's eyes. He stumbled as he dismounted, crashed into the wagon that had been slewed sideways on the bridge, then pulled himself up onto its bed. He was screaming like a madman, expecting a bullet in his belly at any second, but the redcoats were still reloading. He jumped down at them, sabre swinging, and Sergeant Coignet was beside him and then a swarm of pigtailed hussars was jumping over the wagon with pistols flaming and sabres reflecting the dazzling sun. A redcoat was on his knees, hands at his face and blood seeping between his fingers. Another was dead, slumped on the bridge parapet, and the others were going backwards. They did not even have bayonets fixed, and Pailleterie swept a musket aside with his heavy sabre and chopped down at the redcoat, and the man span away, his cheek laid open, and then the other redcoats broke and ran.

"Into the fort!" Pailleterie shouted at his excited men, "into the fort!" The redcoats could wait. The fort must be taken and held until Herault arrived, and he saw there were no gates in the big arch and he ran inside and saw a tall man in a green jacket disappearing though a door. "Up!" He shouted, pointing his men at the courtyard staircase, "up!" A gun banged from the sky and a bullet flattened itself on the stones beside Pailleterie who looked up and saw another green jacketed man silhouetted against the sky, then that man vanished as the hussars ran up the stairs.

Pailleterie hauled a watch from a small pocket of his dolman jacket. He clicked open the domed silver lid and saw there were six hours till Herault arrived, maybe less. He closed the watch, put it away, and bent over, hands on his knees, suddenly tired. My God, though, he had done it! The tip of his sabre was red, and he wiped it on a handful of straw, then was aware that his men were shouting angrily out on the bridge.

He hurried back. Most of his troopers had not needed to dismount and cross the barricade, and those men now milled about at the bridge's southern end. And there they were suffering because a steady fire was coming from a white farmhouse just a couple of hundred paces down the road. Horses were whinnying in pain, men were on the ground, and the damn fire kept coming and it struck Pailleterie that he had seen green jackets, which meant riflemen, and if he did not shelter his men soon then the damned rifles would kill every last one of them.

"Sergeant! Move the wagon! Move it!"

A dozen men heaved the wagon up, thrusting one pair of its wheels onto the bridge's parapet. It was too cumbersome to tip right over the edge, but the dozen men had made a space into which the hussars could spur their horses and so escape across the bridge. "Into the fort!" Pailleterie shouted, "into the fort!" A corporal had rescued the Captain's own horse, and Pailleterie led the beast into the courtyard where it was safe from the rifle fire. Then he opened a saddlebag and took out a tricolour that he gave to Coignet. "Hang it on the battlements, Sergeant. Hang it high."

Hagman and his riflemen had gone down the ladder stairs and now bolted out of the door leading to the storeroom. The French found that entrance a moment too late, but it did not matter. They had seized San Miguel, they had secured the river crossing, and Herault was coming to spread panic along the British supply lines.

And the tricolour flew high above the Tormes.

§§§

It was Sergeant Coignet who found the wine, hundreds of bottles of it, all concealed behind the chipped plaster image of the Virgin Mary that stood in the small shrine across the bridge from the fort. "You want me to break the bottles, sir" He asked Pailleterie.

"Leave them be," Pailleterie said. The wine would make a gift for General Herault. "But make sure no one takes any. If one man gets drunk Sergeant, I'll geld him."

"They'll not touch it, sir," Coignet promised. He was a short, tough man who had never known any life other than the army and within the elite company his word was law. The wine was safe. "Funny place to put wine, though," he told his captain. "Why not in the fort?"

"Maybe they thought the Virgin would protect it?"

"Wine? She might look after milk, sir, but wine?"

"And she didn't protect it," Pailleterie observed, "because it's ours now."

Pailleterie had taken three prisoners. Two were wounded red-coats, one of whom would probably die, while the third was a plump and terrified man in a blue uniform who claimed to be a Major of the Commissary service. His presence was explained by the hoard of French muskets that the hussars had discovered, muskets that would now go back to their proper owners. "You give me your word as a gentleman," Pailleterie asked Tubbs in English, "that you will not try to escape?"

"Of course not," Tubbs said.

"You won't give me your word?"

"No, no! I won't try to escape!" Tubbs stepped nervously away from the pigtailed Frenchman.

"Then you may keep your sword, monsieur," Pailleterie said with a small bow, "and do me the honour of staying inside the fortress."

Not that any of the hussars had much choice in the matter, for whenever they went outside the fort's walls a rifleman would fire. Coignet had narrowly escaped injury when he went to explore the shrine, and two men had died and six had been wounded when Pailleterie had tipped the wagon that had been half-blocking the bridge over the parapet and into the river. Pailleterie regretted the wounding of those two men, but he needed the roadway clear for General Herault's arrival, and so he had led twenty men out of the fort where they immediately came under fire from the farmhouse on the northern bank. "*Vite! Vite!*" Pailleterie had shouted, making sure he was closest to the rifle fire, and then his men had heaved at the wagon, rocking it and finally tipping it over the parapet where it had teetered for a second, splinters driving from its boards where the rifle bullets struck, then it had crashed down into the river. Once the bar-ricade was gone Pailleterie ordered his men to stay inside the fort's walls, even though his Lieutenant, who had been watching the farm-house from the parapet, swore that the riflemen there had now run away. But Pailleterie knew that if they stayed inside the fort his hus-sars and their horses were safe. The British might try to recapture the bridge, but Pailleterie was confident he could thwart them. He had forty of his men lined in the fort's gateway, all armed with pistols, and if the British did run up the road and turn into the arch they would die in a blistering volley.

So the road from the south was open.

General Herault and his small army were coming.

And all Pailleterie needed to do was wait.

§§§

"It was my fault," Sharpe said bitterly.

"I shouldn't have fired so soon," Price admitted.

"I shouldn't have put Pat Harper across the river," Sharpe said. "I should have kept our men together."

Ensign Hickey said nothing, but just looked heartbroken. He had not thought Captain Sharpe could be defeated.

"Bloody hell!" Sharpe swore uselessly. He had pulled his surviving men back to the village where they could shelter behind garden walls. The fort was a hundred paces away across the vineyard, and he had thought about making an attack on it, but he would have to lead his men round to the far side and then through the archway and he guessed the French would be expecting that approach. The storeroom door had been shut, and was doubtless barricaded. Every now and then a black fur hat showed on the parapet as an hussar peered over to make certain the British troops were not planning any mischief. Every glimpse of a pigtailed enemy face prompted a fusillade of rifle and musket fire.

Daniel Hagman, keeping watch from the river bank, reported that the frogs had tipped the cart into the river. "But I got one of the bastards, sir," he said, "and Harris popped another."

"Well done, Dan," Sharpe said morosely, then wondered why the French would clear the barricade away and the answer was depressingly obvious. Because they were expecting more men, that was why. Because the hussars were only holding the bridge long enough to let a flood of bloody Crapauds across the river. Because all hell was about to be loosed on the British supply lines and Captain Richard Sharpe would be blamed. And quite right too, because it was his fault. "Jesus!" Sharpe cursed.

"He doesn't seem to be on our side today," Hagman said mildly.

The only good news was that Harper had brought his men safely

45

back across the Tormes. He had led them a mile westwards and used a fisherman's skiff to ferry them over the river and it was reassuring for Sharpe to have the big Irishman and the twenty rifleman back at his side, but he did not know what he could do with them. Have them killed in a forlorn attack on the fort's gate?

The Scotsman, MacKeon, came and squatted beside Sharpe. He was carrying a musket taken from a dead redcoat and smoking a short foul pipe that he now pointed towards the fort. "It reminds me, Captain," he said, "of that terrible place in India."

Sharpe wondered if MacKeon was drunk. The fort at San Miguel was nothing like Gawilghur. The Indian fort had been built on a clifftop, dizzyingly high above the Deccan plain, while San Miguel was a decaying ruin built beside a river. "It don't look much like Gawilghur to me," Sharpe said sourly.

"Mebbe not," MacKeon said, tapping the pipe out against a stone, "but the pigtailed fellows reckon there's only one way in. And they're guarding that entrance, like as not, but there's always a back way, Captain, always a back way. And you were the laddie that found it at Gawilghur." He pointed the stem of his pipe at the fort. "See that great crack?"

MacKeon was pointing to a jagged fissure that began low on the shadowed western wall then zig-zagged up the stones almost to the parapet. For a moment Sharpe was wondering whether the Scotsman really expected the light company to climb the wall, then saw that, maybe ten or eleven feet above the ground, a whole section of stonework had fallen away. The space looked like a small cave and was half hidden by ivy, but MacKeon was right. It was a back way in, and an agile man could squeeze through the gap, but to what? Sharpe could not remember seeing a hole inside the fort, so where did it lead? "Sergeant Harper?"

"Sir?"

"If a frog shows his head above that parapet, shoot him." The riflemen could keep the French out of sight, and if they were out of sight they could not see what mischief Sharpe planned. He unbuckled his sword belt, let the clumsy weapon drop, and then, with the rifle slung on his shoulder, wriggled between two rows of vines towards the fort's wall. No Frenchman saw him, for he was half hidden by leaves and the enemy were keeping their heads below the parapet. They might have captured the fort, but they were trapped inside it so long as the rifles were outside.

Sharpe reached the base of the fort where grass grew long against the stones. He looked up to where birds flew in and out of their nesting places built in the crumbling masonry, then he reached up and began to climb. It was hard. Much worse than the cliff at Gawilghur. That had been steep, but not vertical, and at Gawilghur there had been bushes that provided handholds. The crack in the fort wall gave plenty of handholds, but it sloped from left to right and Sharpe had to scrabble to find footholds in the old wall, but he hauled himself up, half expecting a pistol to bang above him, and then at last he could grab the ivy's thick trunk and that helped. One good lodgement for his foot and he could thrust himself into the great hole in the wall.

The hole was smaller than it had looked, but Sharpe turned sideways and squeezed between the stones. The tight squeeze made him think of the chimney he had climbed in Copenhagen and he shuddered at that memory, then his rifle caught on the ivy, and his uniform snagged on the edge of the stones and he feared the French must hear him as he pulled himself free and pushed on until his head was inside the fort. A foul stench assailed him, and at first he could see nothing but darkness, then he saw chinks of light above him and heard footsteps on timber and realised that he had entered the space between the store-room's barrel-vaulted stone ceiling and the lowermost timber floor. He wriggled on until he was inside the wall and wondered what he had achieved. There was no way to mount an attack from here. It would take men far too long to climb the wall, and they could only enter one at a time and even when they were inside, what could they do? They would be trapped in a narrowing space between the store-room's ceiling and the newer timber floor above and as his eyes became accustomed to the gloom he saw that the floor beams were oddly ragged, and then he realised he was staring at thousand of bats hanging from the timbers. "Bloody hell," he muttered, and he tried to forget the bats and looked about him and saw that the space was thick with supporting timbers, some quite small, but all placed to support the floors on the curved stone roof that was thick with bat dung. It was the dung that stank so high.

A rifle banged, then another. A Frenchman shouted in alarm high above Sharpe, then another laughed. Sharpe looked out of the cave-like opening and saw two puffs of smoke lingering by the buildings on the far side of the vineyard where his men were sheltering. He pushed back through the crack and raised one finger and then beckoned to let Harper know that he wanted one man to come to him.

Harper sent Perkins who ran at a crouch between the vines to the base of the wall, and again no Frenchman saw the intruder for they were too scared of the rifles. "Can you hear me, Perkins?" Sharpe called, keeping his voice low, and when Perkins nodded Sharpe told him what he wanted, then watched as the boy ran back to the village. Sharpe could only wait now, so he settled inside the hole and listened to the French walking an inch or two above his head. He could smell their horses, smell tobacco smoke, and then he heard English being spoken. "You were not in command here, Major?" A French accented voice asked.

"In overall command, yes, of course," it was Tubbs who answered, "but the defence of the fort, the military defence, was in the hands of a rifle officer. A man called Sharpe."

"He let you down, Major," the Frenchman said. "His men ran like deer!"

"Disgraceful," Tubbs said. "If I'm exchanged, *monsieur,* I shall let the authorities know. But he's a wartime officer, Pailleterie, a wartime officer."

"Aren't we all?" Pailleterie asked.

"Sharpe is up from the ranks," Tubbs said scornfully. "Things like that happen in war, don't you know? A fellow makes a half-decent showing as a sergeant, and next thing they've stitched a yard of braid on his collar and expect him to behave like a gentleman. But they don't satisfy. Ain't brought up to it, y'see?"

"You think so?" Pailleterie asked.

"It's well understood!" Tubbs declared warmly. "If there weren't a shortage of officers then fellows like Sharpe wouldn't be officers. They'd stay where they belong. Down in the gutter, eh? But a few have to be promoted and all they do is take to drink. Take to drink and make a pickle out of things. I told Sharpe, I told him straight. The French will be coming, I said, but he wouldn't listen. But what can one expect, eh? The fellow came up from the ranks and he really ain't up to scratch, ain't up to it at all."

"I came up from the ranks," Pailleterie said mildly and Tubbs blustered for a few seconds, then was silent. The Frenchman laughed. "More wine, Major? It will console you in defeat."

Bastard, Sharpe thought, meaning Tubbs, not the damned frog, then he wriggled back into the opening because Perkins was slithering back between the vines, this time accompanied by Cooper and Harris who both dragged huge bundles wrapped in blankets. Perkins had a makeshift rope made from a half dozen musket slings and he stood close to the wall and threw one end up to Sharpe who caught it on the second attempt and then there was a pause while the other end was attached to the first big bundle.

It took five or six minutes to haul both bundles up. It was not lifting them that took the time, but manoeuvring their awkward bulk through the narrow crack and Sharpe was horribly aware of the Frenchmen so close overhead and of the bats that were shuddering now as they sensed activity close by.

"Might I take the air on the parapet?" Tubbs asked, so close that Sharpe jumped when the major spoke.

"Of course, *monsieur*," Pailleterie answered, "but I shall accompany you to keep you safe. If you show your head by the western parapet, bang!"

Sharpe listened to the feet climbing the ladders, and then he began piling the contents of the two bundles between the short, slanting timbers that propped up the floor. Perkins had done well. There was straw, kindling and even a stoppered clay jar of lamp oil that a villager had donated, and Sharpe soaked the wood and straw in lamp oil and then, with a grimace of disgust, scooped his right forefinger through a sticky patch of bat dung.

His rifle was loaded, so he dared not strike a spark with its lock until he had blocked the touch-hole and so, stooping near the hole in the wall so he could see properly, he opened the frizzen and dabbed the bat dung into the rifle's touch-hole. Now a spark in the pan could not connect with the powder in the rifle's barrel.

He took out a rifle cartridge, tore it open and discarded the bullet. He sprinkled most of the powder onto the kindling, but he kept a pinch that he put on top of the torn paper which he trapped inside the rifle's lock. He cocked the weapon, flinching at the loud click and then, hoping that no Frenchman would think it odd to hear a misfire beneath his feet, pulled the trigger.

The spark flashed and the powder fizzed, but the paper did not catch fire, so Sharpe had to tear another cartridge open for more gunpowder. He placed it in the lock, cocked the gun again and pulled the trigger.

This time the paper flickered with small fizzing blue flames, and he took it from the lock, held it downwards so the flames would grow as they climbed the paper and when it was really burning and the first bats were flickering in panic around his head, he put the paper down among the loose straw. He waited as the flames caught hold, as the gunpowder in the kindling sparked and hissed, and then the fire reached some lamp oil and the flames leaped up the pile of kindling and the smoke began to curl in the dark space that was filling with fluttering bats.

Sharpe forced himself out through the hole in the wall, tearing his coat on a protruding stone. The smoke had thickened with incredible speed and was boiling out over his head, while bats were squeaking and skittering all around him. He reached for the ivy and let himself fall. For a second he hung from the ivy's trunk, staring up at the mix of bats and smoke that poured from the gap in the wall, and then a Frenchman shouted and a rifle cracked, then another, and the ivy was peeling off the wall, lowering Sharpe, and he just let go and fell heavily onto the vines. A pistol cracked and a puff of dust showed a couple of feet to his right where the small bullet struck the ground.

He was winded, but there did not seem to be any bones broke. He picked up his rifle and half ran, half limped towards the village. A dozen rifles fired and Sharpe heard the balls crack against stone, and then he was safe in the ditch and Pat Harper leaned down and hauled him up into the vegetable garden where the Light Company sheltered.

"Let them piss on that fire, eh, sir?" Harper said, nodding towards the hole in the fort wall that now spewed a thick grey smoke.

"Best thing to do with rats," Mister MacKeon said, "burn them out."

Sharpe cupped his hands. "Harry?"

"Sir?" Lieutenant Price answered.

"Redcoats in two ranks, if you please. Muskets loaded and bayonets fixed. Pat?"

"Sir?"

"Rifles to follow me. We charge on my command, Mister Price."

"Yes, sir!"

So long as the buggers did not extinguish the fire, Sharpe thought, he still had a chance of winning this fight.

§§§

The smoke sifted up through the floorboards, and for a short while no one noticed, but then Sergeant Coignet raised the alarm and by then the lowest wooden floor was thick with smoke, though there were no flames to be seen.

"Water!" Pailleterie shouted. "Get it from the river! Make a chain! Sergeant Gobel! A dozen men to keep the horses quiet! Make a chain! Use your hats!"

A chain of men could pass colbacks filled with river water up from the bank, through the arch and up the ladder to the first floor, but as soon as the first men reached the bank and leaned down to scoop up water, a rifle fired, and then another, and there were two dead hussars, and a third man was wounded. It took Sergeant Coignet valuable moments to reorganise his human chain to scoop water from the farther side of the bridge where the stone of the northernmost arch would protect his men, and by then it was already too late.

The fire had not yet broken through the floorboards, but it was feasting on the short dry timbers that supported the floor, and the curved barrel-roof of the store-room made a natural horizontal chimney that filled with air and dying bats to fan the flames. The smoke thickened so that when the first water came up the ladder, and there was precious little of it for the fur hats leaked atrociously, Pailleterie could only throw the water into the choking smoke and hope it did some good. He could hear the fire roaring like a furnace beneath his feet and he could feel the heat coming through the planks. One of the collapsible canvas buckets with which the hussars watered their horses came up the human chain and Pailleterie hurled its contents into the smoke.

The water hissed, but it did nothing, for the whole floor was now under siege, and in a few seconds the flames broke through in a half dozen places and the draught now whipped the fire up into the tangle of dry timbers that filled the western half of the fort. The flames climbed the ladders, snaked up beams, burned at the thin partitions

51

and the ever thickening smoke forced the hussars back. The horses were whinnying in panic. "Gobel!" Pailleterie shouted, "get the horses onto the northern bank! Go! Go!"

The horses were led out of the gate and, seeing freedom, they bolted across the bridge towards the olive groves. The flames were crackling and leaping, filling the space inside the fort with an unbearable heat and churning smoke. "Onto the bridge!" Pailleterie shouted, "pistols! Sergeant Coignet! On the bridge! Face north! Lieutenant! Where are the prisoners? Fetch them!"

Smoke-blackened hussars stumbled out of the arch. The square tower was now one vast chimney and the dry timbers were being consumed in a constant roar that billowed smoke high into the sky. Flames leaped twenty, thirty feet above the parapet. Coignet was thrusting men into ranks, but they were nervous for the furnace roar was right beside them and smouldering embers were dropping among them, and somewhere inside the fort a man was screaming terribly because he had been trapped. The wounded redcoats were carried out and placed on the grass beyond the shrine.

And then the rifle fire began. Shot after shot, coming from the north, from a ditch there, and hussars were thrown back or bent over.

"We'll charge them!" Pailleterie pushed into the front rank and drew his sabre. The rifles were not so far away, maybe sixty yards, and he would sabre the bastards into the dry ground. "Draw sabres!"

There were some sixty men on the bridge and they drew their sabres.

It was Pailleterie's last chance to hold the bridge.

And Sharpe shouted "Fire!"

§§§

"Fire!" Sharpe shouted, and Lieutenant Price's redcoats who had run from the village to form two ranks across the road, fired a volley southwards into the hussars and there was suddenly blood on the road, and men crumpling and staggering.

"Charge!" Sharpe shouted. "Come on!" And he was running ahead of them, sword drawn, and the tower was belching smoky flames to his right and the hussars were edging backwards, those that still stood, and Sharpe was filled with an utter fury. How dare these bastards have defeated him? And all he wanted to do now was to kill them, to take his revenge, but they were running now, fleeing from the glitter of bayonets. Not one man stood. The wounded hussars crawled on the road, the dead lay still, but the living fled back to the southern bank to escape the vengeful infantry.

And Captain Pailleterie was also filled with a single-minded rage. How dare these bastards deny him his victory? All night he had ridden, and he had evaded the picquets in the sierra's foothills and defeated the infantry garrison of a fort with cavalrymen. With cavalrymen! Men had received the *Legion d'honneur* for less, and now the bastards had come back from the dead to cheat him of his glory. "Coignet! Coignet! Come back! Hussars! Turn! Turn! For the Emperor."

Bugger the Emperor. It was pride that checked them, not the Emperor. They were an elite company, and when they saw the Captain turning back onto the bridge, at least half of them followed and so two bands of angry men, their pride at stake, clashed above the Tormes.

"Now kill the bastards!" Sharpe shouted and he was filled with a ridiculous elation that the crapauds were going to fight after all, and he scythed the heavy-cavalry sword down onto the neck of a Frenchman, twisted the blade free as he kicked the falling man in the face, then stabbed the bloody blade forward. It was sabres against bayonets, and wild as a tavern brawl. It was gutter fighting with government issue weapons. Stab and slash and snarl and kick, and in truth the two sides were too close together for either to have an advantage. The redcoats were crammed against hussars and did not have room to bring their bayonets back, and when the hussars cut down with sabres they risked having their sword arms seized. Some men fired pistols, and that would create a small gap, but it would immediately be filled. A redcoat collapsed across the parapet, his face pale and belly slit open by a sabre. An hussar went down, his skull crushed by Sharpe's sword that had cut straight through the fur colback. Sergeant Coignet tried to reach the tall rifle officer, but he tripped on a dead body and the rifle officer kicked him in the face, kicked him again, and Coignet tried to roll over, spitting out teeth, to stab his sabre up into the bastard's groin, but Sharpe was quicker and stabbed down first. The sword blade scraped on ribs, then broke through to splash blood onto Sharpe's boots. Pailleterie was carving space for himself by slashing his sabre from side to side, and Sharpe stepped back from Coignet's body and wrenched the sword free from the Sergeant's corpse, and then leaped back because Pailleterie had lunged, but a sabre is a poor lunging weapon and Sharpe smacked it aside with his sword and ran at the hussar captain, just ran at him, and gripped him in a bear hug and thrust him against the parapet and then pushed.

Pailleterie shouted as he fell into the river, then another voice shouted, much louder. "The hell out the way! Out the God damned way!" And Sergeant Harper had arrived with his seven-barrelled gun, the vicious cluster of barrels held at his hip and the redcoats twisted aside as the big Irishman came straight up the bridge's centre. "Bastards!" Harper shouted, then pulled the trigger and it was as if a cannon had been fired. Blood misted over the Tormes, and Harper was charging into the bloody space he had made, swinging the stubby seven-barrelled gun like a club. He was chanting in Irish, lost in an ancient saga when heroes had counted their enemy dead in the scores.

And the hussars, their beloved captain gone, gave ground. "Keep after them!" Sharpe snarled, "don't let them breathe! Kill them!" And men stepped over bodies, slipped in blood and carried the bayonets forward and Sharpe broke a sabre clean in two with a cut of the sword and then stabbed his blade into a pigtailed face, and suddenly the French really did break. They broke and ran. Ran back the way they had come.

"Hold it there!" Sharpe called. "Stop! Stop!"

The bridge was his. The French were running. A dripping Pailleterie was clambering up the southern bank, but the fight had been drenched out of him and his men were running.

"Form ranks!" Sharpe shouted. Form ranks, count the dead, bind up the wounded and then he looked south and his mouth dropped open. "Bloody hell," he said.

"God save Ireland," Patrick Harper spoke beside him.

Because every bloody cavalryman in France was on the road. All the Emperor's horses and all the Emperor's men with lances, swords and sabres. In blue coats and green coats, in white coats and brown coats. With plumes and braid and lace and pelisses and sabretaches and glitter. The polished blades caught the sun like a field of steel.

And all those horsemen were coming straight at the South Essex Light Company.

"God save Ireland," Harper said again.

"Back!" Sharpe said, "back!" Back to the northern side of the bridge. Not that retreating would do him much good, but it might give him time to think.

To think about what? Death?

Just what the hell could he do?

§§§

General Herault did not have all his men, for some of the horses had simply collapsed during the long night march, but he had close to twelve hundred cavalrymen and he had come down from the Sierra de Gredos to see the fort at San Miguel de Tormes belching smoke like a furnace and to see his beloved elite company of hussars thrust off the bridge by a ragtag collection of redcoats and greenjackets.

But there was only a handful of British infantry and one glance at the northern bank showed Herault that there were no more British troops at hand. No artillery, no cavalry, no more infantry, just the one small band of men who even as he watched scuttled back over the bridge's hump to form a double rank at the far end of the roadway. The riflemen were scattering along the bank, plainly intending to rake the flank of any cavalry charge with their horribly accurate marksmanship.

So that was what stood between him and victory. Two ranks and a handful of grasshoppers. That was what the French called the riflemen, grasshoppers. The bastards were always darting about in the grass, sniping away, then moving on. *Sauterelles*.

Herault paused. No need to go bald-headed at the bridge. Even a handful of redcoats could do damage in the confined space of a bridge's roadway, and two dead horses dropped between the parapets would make a horribly effective barricade. No, these *rosbifs* and sauterelles must be thinned out and then he would release a murderous company of Polish lancers at them. Infantry hated lancers. Herault loved them.

He summoned his green-jacketed dragoons first. Dragoons were supposed to be mounted infantry and they all carried longarms as well as swords, and Herault had three hundred of them in his force. "Dismount your men," he ordered the dragoon colonel, "and make a skirmish line. Get them close to the river and smother those bastards with fire." He reckoned the dragoons could silence the riflemen, though the redcoats could probably find shelter by crouching under the bridge parapets. Which is where he wanted them.

"You want me to charge the bridge on foot?" The dragoon Colonel asked.

"I shall charge the bridge," Herault said. The dragoons would make the redcoats cower behind the parapets and Herault would burst across the bridge with the dreaded Polish horsemen.

The dragoons dismounted, leaving their horses with the hussars, and ran forward with their carbines. Herault let them get on with their job while he trotted his horse to where the Poles waited in their dark blue uniforms fronted with yellow and with their square-sided, black leather, yellow topped tsapka hats. Their lances were newly sharpened, each long double-edged blade as keen as a razor. He chose a company that wore the single white epaulettes to show they were an elite unit and he borrowed a lance from a trooper in another company. It was an ash pole, fourteen feet long, with a narrow steel blade projecting another eighteen inches. Herault had seen a lancer at the full gallop take the top off a hard-boiled egg, and the eggcup had not even quivered as the lance blade struck and cut. "In a few moments," he told the Poles, pausing to let his words be translated, "we shall cross the bridge and we shall kill them all." He would lead them, because that was the tradition in the French army. Had not General Bonaparte made his name on the bridge at Arcola? So now Herault would add another bridge to the legends of France.

The dragoons had opened a galling fire across the Tormes and Herault, twisting in his saddle, saw the *sauterelles* running back from their fire. He pushed his right hand through the wrist loop that was fastened at the lance's midpoint.

It was time to swat the enemy aside.

Time to win.

§§§

Bloody hell, Sharpe thought, but what to do? If his men stood up they exposed themselves to the galling fire of the three hundred dragoons, and if they stayed crouching they could not see over the bridge's hump. They could fire one volley when the French came, but by then the big horses would be within forty feet and, though the volley might kill the leading cavalrymen, the dead and dying horses would slide forward on the roadway to smash their weight into the redcoats. Sharpe had seen the first French square break at Garcia Hernandez because the French held their fire an instant too long and the dead weight of the slaughtered horses had broken through the square's face like a battering ram. He stood, attracting a whistling volley of dragoon fire, but he endured it long enough to see a squadron of lancers trotting towards the road. "Bloody lancers," he said. He hated lancers.

He needed to barricade the bridge, but the wagon was in the river and any of the fort's timbers that might have been useful were now part of an inferno. The smoke and embers whirled around Sharpe. The fort's upper floors had collapsed, spewing sparks high into the cloudless sky and the heat of the fire was like a furnace.

Mister MacKeon was crouching beside the wayside shrine and now beckoned Sharpe who crossed to him and the Scotsman jerked a thumb through the iron-grille gate that protected the Virgin. "Your answer's there, Mister Sharpe," he said.

Prayer? Sharpe wondered, then he looked past the chipped plaster saint and saw to his astonishment that the back of the chapel was piled with hundreds of bottles of wine that Harper had been ordered to smash. "Have you ever heard of caltrops?" MacKeon asked.

Caltrops. Sharpe had not only heard of them, he had used them once in the narrow streets of Santiago de Compostela. A caltrop was a four pointed star of metal spikes that, scattered with hundreds of others on the ground, served to disable a cavalry charge. The caltrops' spikes went through the soft part of the hoof and no horse could keep going through the agony, and Harper's disobedience had suggested a makeshift form of caltrops.

"Harper! Harris! Cooper! Perkins!" Sharpe bellowed towards the vineyard where the riflemen had taken shelter. "Come here! Now! Fast!"

A trumpet sounded on the southern road and the lancers lowered their blades. General Herault walked his tired horse to the front of the squadron. The dragoons blasted a volley that ricocheted off the bridge parapet or flattened its bullets against the fort's stonework. If that bugger of a wall collapses, Sharpe thought, it could crush his men, but there was no time to worry about that. Only time for Harper to finish his work.

The four riflemen had sprinted over the field and dropped beside Sharpe as the bullets whipped overhead. "Every damn bottle, Pat," Sharpe said, "is to be broken, just as I bloody ordered you."

"Now, sir?" Harper asked, staring at Sharpe as though he were mad. "You want us to do it now?"

"Throw them up onto the bridge," Sharpe said. "Right in the bridge's centre. Do it now! Do it fast! Just bloody do it!"

Harris and Perkins crouched inside the shrine and pushed bottles out of the door, and Harper, Sharpe and Cooper hurled them up onto the bridge's hump. MacKeon helped, and then two of the redcoats came to assist because there were so many bottles. Hundreds! Harper must have saved four hundred! Doubtless he had hoped Sharpe would not see them, and then he would have distributed the wine among the Light Company or, more likely, sold it to the villagers and Sharpe was now damned grateful for the Irishman's disobedience. "Hurry!" He shouted, for the trumpet had sounded again and he could hear the thump of hooves.

They hurled the bottles until the bridge ran with wine. Wine that diluted the drying blood and trickled past the dead bodies left on the roadway. But it was not the wine that would save Sharpe, but the thick layer of broken green glass that was beginning to build up in the bridge's centre, and still he threw more bottles that smashed apart in fountains of red, and every broken bottle left a handful of razor sharp glass scraps just like those that rich folk mortared into the summits of their high walls to keep out thieves and Sharpe, in his youth, had been bloodied by more than one such trap. Broken glass. Bloody sharp stuff, horrid stuff, and Harris and Perkins backed out of the shrine, their arms filled with the last bottles that they hurled up onto the bridge and now the hooves were a thunder to fill the air and shake the ground, and the curb chains and scabbard chains clinked and Sharpe stood to see the lances coming straight at him and even the dragoons had stopped firing to watch the Poles slaughter their way across the bridge.

"Stand up!" Sharpe shouted at his redcoats. "Present!" The muskets came up into mens' shoulders. Their bayonets, many still red with blood, pointed towards the bridge crest that glittered with a thick bed of shattered green glass.

And the lancers were in a line now, narrowing to cross the bridge at a flying gallop and the Elysian Fields were loud with the sound of hooves and the blare of the trumpet driving the long lances onwards, and Sharpe drew his sword, tugging it hard because the blood drying on the blade had crusted to the inside of the scabbard. Some of the dragoons had opened fire. A redcoat staggered, his musket dropping and Sergeant Huckfield pulled him back out of the front rank. "Close up! Close up!" The litany of battle. "Close up!" Harper's riflemen were firing at the dragoons and the leading lancers were just on the bridge.

"Fire! Sharpe shouted, and his thirty muskets flamed and smoked and he had an impression of a horse falling and screaming. "Reload! Fast!" He shouted, "reload!" The sound of hooves were still loud on the stone and Sharpe ran to one side to see past the musket's thick smoke and an hussar was leading the charge, but this hussar had a lance and he reached the bridge's crest and there his horse reared, and the horse was screaming, green light flashing off its flailing front hooves, and a second horse was sliding in the glass, shaking, its rider desperately trying to regain control, and then a third horse reached the broken glass and it too reared up. The lancers piled in behind, unable to get past the panicking horses. Those horses were in screaming agony, blood dripping from hooves, and Sharpe looked at his redcoats, watching the ramrods go back into the musket hoops. "Present!" He shouted. The muskets came up again as a dragoon's bullet whiplashed past Sharpe's shako. "Fire!" He called, and this time the three leading horses went down, struck by the volley, and the bridge was blocked. Two of the horses died within seconds, but the third lay on its side and screamed as it beat its hooves against the glass that had defeated the charge.

Sharpe bulled through the ranks and ran up onto the bridge that was slippery with wine. The hussar was trapped beneath his horse, and grimacing because he had fallen among the broken glass, but he tried to lift the lance as Sharpe approached, but Sharpe knocked the lance aside, then grabbed the hussar by the collar of his brown coat and just dragged him away from his horse. Glass crunched under Sharpe's boots. The hussar screamed as his hip was pulled through the shattered bottles, then Sharpe tugged him clear and pulled the man's pistol from its holster. He cocked it, aimed it, fired and the screaming horse gave a shudder and died. Then Sharpe pushed his prisoner back down the bridge. "Harry!" He shouted at Lieutenant Price. "Take the redcoats up to the dead horses. That's your new barricade! Ensign?" He called for Hickey, because he knew the ensign spoke some French and he wanted to persuade the enemy to have a truce while the wounded were collected. The real point of the truce was to buy time for the reinforcements from Salamanca to arrive. "Ensign!" He shouted again.

"Dead, sir," Harper said. "Hit by a dragoon."

"God damn, another bloody ensign gone." Sharpe said. He tugged the lance off his prisoner, breaking the wrist-strap, then pulled out the Frenchman's sabre. "Harris? You speak frog. Find out what the hell these bastards are doing here. And give the bastard a kicking if he won't talk. Then tell him we want a truce to treat the wounded."

Then there were more hooves, another trumpet, and Sharpe whipped round and saw there was no need for a truce because the reinforcements had already come. He stared north and saw horsemen in blue and yellow, a whole regiment of horsemen galloping on the road from Salamanca, their horses white with sweat because they had ridden so hard and Teresa was alongside the leading officer who raised a hand and grinned at Sharpe as he curbed his horse.

"Captain Lossow," Sharpe said, reaching up to shake the German's hand.

Captain Lossow of the King's German Legion looked at the blood and wine on the bridge, and at the dragoons who were trudging back towards their horses, and then at the great mass of French cavalry who were stalled in the fields beyond. "There must be a thousand men over there, Richard," Lossow said.

"You want to go and play with them? You'll have to let me clear the bridge of glass first."

"We shall wait here," Lossow said, swinging down from his saddle. "We have a battalion of infantry coming and a battery of guns. But it looks as if you managed without us."

"We coped," Sharpe said, smiling up at Teresa. "We coped."

Tubbs had been trapped in the burning fort and he was dead, and the captured French muskets were now nothing but a twisted mass of molten metal. Good for nothing, MacKeon said, but Sharpe knew he would never have won this scrap if it had not been for MacKeon. "I owe you," he said.

"To hell and away," the Scotsman said. "I just remembered how you managed at Gawilghur, Mister Sharpe, and reckoned you could manage again."

Pierre Ducos appeared that evening with the French infantry, but Herault's brave idea was defeated, and now a battery of British field guns and a line of redcoats defended the bridge beside the smoking fort. Herault himself was a prisoner, captured, Captain Pailleterie said, by a rifleman called Sharpe. Ducos spat. The fools! The French cavalry had captured the bridge and then lost it! The incompetent fools. "You will be punished for this, Pailleterie," he promised, "punished!" And then he ordered General Michaud to turn his infantrymen about and march them away south, and he took out his small notebook and crossed out the recommendation for General Herault's promotion, and added Pailleterie's name with a cross beside it, and then the name of the British rifle officer who had cheated him of victory. Sharp, he wrote, not knowing there should be an 'e'. A name to remember, but then, Ducos forgot nothing.

Sharpe watched the enemy leave. He stood with Teresa on the crest of the bridge at San Miguel de Tormes, and watched the French retreat. And it was his company that had turned them back. "I was lucky," he said softly. "Didn't deserve to win."

"Of course you deserved to win," Teresa said.

"It was MacKeon." Sharpe said. "He reminded me of what we did at Gawilghur. And then it was Pat Harper, disobeying orders as usual."

"There was a battle," Teresa said, "in Spain, and we won."

"No," Sharpe said, putting an arm about her shoulders. "It weren't a battle, love. Just a skirmish." Just a skirmish, but the French had lost and their general was Sharpe's prisoner. And too many men had died, and that was Sharpe's fault, but the army would only remember that Captain Sharpe had stopped the frogs and so, for the moment, his career was safe and the French would abandon Madrid and Wellington could keep marching north. And all because Sharpe had fought a skirmish and he had won. It was Sharpe's skirmish.